Jackrabbit Street

JACKRABBIT STREET

Joe Welsh

thistledown press

©Joe Welsh, 2003
All rights reserved

No part of this publication may be reproduced or transmitted in any form or by any means, graphic, electronic or mechanical, including photocopying, recording, or any information storage and retrieval system, without permission in writing from the publisher. Requests for photocopying of any part of this book shall be directed in writing to Access Copyright, 1 Yonge Street, Suite 1900, Toronto, Ontario, M5E 1E5.

National Library of Canada Cataloguing in Publication Data

Welsh, Joseph, 1946-
Jackrabbit Street / Joseph Welsh.

(New leaf editions. Series eight)
ISBN 1-894345-57-6

I. Title. II. Series.
PS8595.E575J32 2003   C813'.6   C2003-911116-4

Cover photograph by Allison Muri
Book and cover design by J. Forrie
Typeset by Thistledown Press

Thistledown Press Ltd.
633 Main Street
Saskatoon, Saskatchewan, S7H 0J8
www.thistledown.sk.ca

Thistledown Press gratefully acknowledges the financial assistance of the Canada Council for the Arts, the Saskatchewan Arts Board, and the Government of Canada through the Book Publishing Industry Development Program for its publishing program.

ACKNOWLEDGEMENTS

Special thanks to:

My editor, Judy Krause.
Curtis Petit for the trip home and the photos and sketches.
Janice Bellerose for being tough and crazy and making me laugh.
Danny Brooks for beer and philosophy.
My sister, Billie, my creative language consultant.
Maria Campbell, who didn't just open the door for us — she kicked the damn thing down.
My sisters, Cec, Billie, Norma, Madeline and Pauline, and my brother, Dan, for carrying me. I know I was a real load.
My storytellers and teachers, who gave me their blessings and permission to write these stories: Joe and Irene Moran, Harriette Pelletier, Margaret Desjarlais, Frank "Fringo" Desjarlais, Louis Brabant, Pete Johnson, Leonard Pambrun, Wannie Fisher, Alec Desmarais, Albert Bellerose, Martin Aubichon, and many others.

With love, respect, and gratitude.

CONTENTS

9	The Making of a Half Breed Bandit
12	St. Pierre and the Bandit
14	Why Rocky Poisson Didn't Join the Army
15	The Bootlegger — Part One
16	Roo Garoo
18	The Burden of Gratitude
21	John Henry Rainville
23	St. Pierre's Grandaughter
24	Janvier's Lullaby
25	The Army Worms
26	The First Communion of Cecile Annette Marie Magdelaine St. Pierre — Part One
27	The First Communion of Cecile Annette Marie Magdelaine St. Pierre — Part Two
28	Le Chien Du Pere Beaulieu
29	Janvier Goes to Confession
30	Janvier Makes a Picnic
31	Janvier's Cousin
32	The Bonspiel
33	Hungry Half Breed Song

34	Half Breed Breakfast
35	Half Breed Air Conditioning
36	How They Make Holy Water
37	The 1949 Election
38	How *Kokum* Emily and *Mussom* Zachary Brought Thanksgiving To Crooked Lake
40	The Bootlegger — Part Two
42	Gunther Primeau
44	The German Woman
46	'Ti Boy — Part One
48	'Ti Boy — Part Two
50	Q Pontoon
51	The English Patient
54	Mary Margaret Francine Striker Jones
57	Seven-Toed Pete
59	Little Petey
62	The Seasons
63	*Mon Cousin*
64	Pee Wee

"Its inhabitants are, as the man once said, whores, pimps, gamblers and sons of bitches, by which he meant Everybody. Had the man looked through another peep- hole he might have said, Saints and angels and martyrs and holy men, and he would have meant the same thing.

— John Steinbeck, *Cannery Row*

THE MAKING OF A HALF BREED BANDIT

Rocky Poisson work for other guys all the time. Cutting fence, digs a well once in a while. He do everthing. He don't make lot of money but he always have a job an' he can feed himself, an' he can always buy a guy a beer once in a while. But Depression come an' lot of guys can't afford to pay a man. Lot of guys have to go long ways to find work, but Poisson he don't want to go away from home. He find a little bit of work sometimes an' he pick up beer bottles an' soft drink bottles along the road. An' he can feed himself still. He trap gophers an' squirrels, prairie chickens an' pigeons. But he have a girlfriend, Rose Adelle Deuxchapeaux, an' he can't take her to picture show an' can't buy her no presents.

One day he come to visit me an' he tell me he's going to be bandit an' rob trains, "Just like Jesse James." He tell me his grandfather use to ride with Jesse James an' he come up here after Northfield because he don't want to get hung. A few guys do that. Guys who ride with Jesse James, the Daltons, Butch Cassidy, they come across an' settle down.

Anyways, Poisson he tell me he wants to be bandit an' he's going to start next week. So me I tell him, "Hollasmokesboy you going to need a horse. You can't go rob a train running after it on foot." So he tell me he don't think about that but he's going to make a plan.

So on the way home he pass the train station an' there's two cream cans there. Empty. So the bugger he steal them an' he go an' trade them to Norbert Delorme for a old horse. Next day he come riding up to my place, an' the poor horse he look like nobody feed him for a few days. An' Poisson he have a hanky wrap around his face an' he's holding the horse by the mane. He's got no bridle. No lines. No saddle. An' he tell me, "What time the train does it go by?"

Ah Diable, I start to laugh an' I tell him, "Hollasmokes Poisson, hownahell you going to rob a train with that old horse? I bet you me I can run faster than him. Besides, you got no gun. You got no bridle. No lines. No saddle. Hownahell you going to hold on to your horse if you got to hold on to couple bags of money at the same time? You're not going to scare nobody like that. A ban Christ, a ban Christ, the train guys they's going to laugh at you."

So he go away an' couple days later he come riding up again. This time he have a bridle a saddle an' lines. Everthing. He even have a six-shooter, but the horse he still don't look too good. I ask him wherenahell he get all that stuff, an' he tell me there's a rodeo at Indian Head, an' there's a bunch of cowboys there an' they's all drunk so he rob them. Then he says, "The train? What time it goes by?" I tell him 1:00 maybe 1:30. So he tell me, "Adios amigo," an' he ride away.

Well boy. The train it come an' it stop at the station an' after a few minutes it pull out. An' you won't believe it. Hey hey maudit crapeau! Before it get going too fast, that crazy bugger Poisson he's chasing after it on that poor old horse. He has his hanky wrap around his face an' have his six-shooter out an' he start to shoot at the train. Pan! Pan! Pan! But a little gun like that it's not going to hurt a train. But never mind. It's a goddam freight train he's trying to rob! An' that poor horse he's getting tired pretty fast but Poisson he don't care. So all at once the train driver, he throw a lump of coal an' it hit Poisson on the head an' knock him off the horse.

Hey hey crapeau! Talk about laugh. Everbody in town see this an' poor Poisson he sit there on the ground an' he swears like a mad farmer. An' his horse he bugger off an' he can't find him. It take three days an' finally Norbert Delorme bring him back. The poor horse I guess he miss his pasture an' he don't have to catch a train before he gets fed. An' Poisson he have a lump on his head for a few days.

But you know. After that he still try to rob people. But everbody know it's him an' nobody's ascared of him. So after a while he get tired an' he try an' trade back to Norbert Delorme the horse for his cream cans. But Delorme he won't do it. Finally Poisson he have to give

Delorme the horse, the saddle, the bridle an' lines, an' the gun before he can get back his two cream cans. So now he's got two cream cans an' he can't do nothing with them. Everbody knows he steal them. So he put them back at the station an' he try an' figger out what else he can do to make money.

An' Rose Adelle Deuxchapeau? One day a cowboy come from Indian Head. Says somebody steal his saddle an' bridle an' gun. Well she don't say nothing. An' he's a handsome guy so she go away with him to a rodeo someplace.

It's last time anybody from around here see her.

St. Pierre and the Bandit

One day me I am cutting wood, the other side the lake over by the seminary. About eleven, eleven thirty in the morning I see a guy come riding up on a horse. Soon as he get closer I see he have a hanky wrap round his face. Just like Jesse James. He have a gun too but right now me, I know it is Rocky Poisson. He come riding up to me an' he pull out his gun an' he tell me, "Okay boy, hands up and give it to me all yer money."

So me I put up my hands an' I tell him, "*Kitchisk* Poisson, I am a Half Breed, I got no money. Go rob a white guy or a priest." Besides, I still have my hands up an' I can't give him the money like that. I have three dollar in my pocket too but I am not telling him that.

So Poisson he tell me now, "Okay half breed pull dem down yer pants." I look at him an' I look at his gun an' I say to myself, " St.Pierre you're going to die sooner or later but old Janvier he still owe you three dollar an' bottle of whiskey, an' you don't want to die sober an' broke." So I pull them down my pants.

Next Poisson he tell me, "Okay now squat down an' make *mishi*." Me I start figgering, "I am going to die sooner or later an' the gun she's not very big but a guy shoot you enough time you're going to be dead just the same. But I am not going to die with my pants down." So I squat down an' make a big *mishi*. Good thing I have lot of coffee an' grens for breakfast.

That crazy goddam Poisson now he tell me, "Okay boy, eat." An' me again I tell him, "*Kitchisk*." He look at his gun an' he look at me an' he tell me, "EAT." Maudit Padue boy, me I worry now. I look at him an' I see he have a mean look on his face an' I am too ascared to ask him if I can first wipe my ass, an' I figger, "You're going to die some day anyway but not with dirty ass." So I eat. Wha wha hiy my boy!

Old Poisson he look at me an' he start to laugh. Muffwey he laugh. He laugh so goddam hard he drop it on the ground his gun an' he fall down, an' he start rolling around an' tears start coming out his eyes.

Right away me I tell myself, "*Maudit Culvert!* Poisson he's going to go back to town an' tell everbody I eat my own shit. *Ah Diable!* I am going to have to kill him before I let him do that." So I jump an' I grab it his gun an' I am just about ready to shoot him but I get a better idea an' I tell him, "Okay Poisson get up an' pull them down your pants."

Poisson he look at me with shit all over my face an' he figger he better not make me provoke no more, so he get up an' he pull them down his pants.

So next I tell him, "Okay Poisson squat down an' make *mishi*." He look at me an' he figger he better not argue with a guy who have a gun an' just finish eating his own shit, so he squat down, an' this time he make a *mishi*. I think he have lot of coffee an' grens for breakfast too.

Poisson he is not that stupid he don't know what is coming next an' he try to talk like a tough guy an' he tell me, "No goddam way St. Pierre, I ain't eatin no shit. Yer gonna have to shoot me first."

So me I say, "Okay Poisson." An' I put a bullet right between his legs. Close enough to circumcise him just about. So now he know I mean business an' he get down an' he eat.

I look at him for a while an' I start to laugh. Sacrament my boy, it is the funniest goddam thing I ever see. I laugh so goddam hard I start to roll on the ground an' I even piss on my pants. Poisson he start laffing like a bugger again too.

Pretty soon we stop, an' Poisson he get two bottle of whiskey from his gunny sack an' we walk down to the lake an' wash the shit off our face, an' we have a couple of drinks to take the taste of shit out our mouth then we go an' sit down. We laugh some more an' we drink some more, an' pretty soon we are drunk, an' we pass out an' we go to sleep.

Anyways boy, that is the time I have lunch with Rocky Poisson, the Half Breed Bandit.

Why Rocky Poisson Didn't Join the Army

One day some army guys come to town. They want to get some of the young guys to join up. So Janvier tell Rocky Poisson, "You should join up boy. They feed you an' pay you an' everthing. Plus you don't have to steal an' you don't have to shit in the bush no more." Then he tell him, "Lot of girls they like a guy who have on a uniform an' have money in his pocket." Poisson he think it's a good idea about them girls. 'Specially since Rose Adelle Deuxchapeaux go away with that cowboy from Indian Head. So he tell Janvier he's going to join up.

Well boy, a couple hours pass an' he come back an' he don't look too good. So Janvier tell him, "What's wrong boy?"

Poisson tell him, "Well I get to dat recruitment place an' dey have four, five guys der. Firs' ting, I have to fill out piece of paper den one of duh guys der, he's a doctor I guess, he tell me to cover one eye an' read what is on a cardboard on duh wall. Den I cover odder eye an' do same ting.

Den he tell me to take dem off my clothes an' he hand me little bottle an' he tell me piss in it. It's a damn small bottle too boy. I bet you even a gopher can fill it up.

So den he have a little flash light an' he shine it in my eyes an' up my nose an' in my ears. An' couple odder places too. Den he grab me by my poche an' he tell me cough. An' after he finish he tell me I can put dem back on my clothes.

So after dat I have to see nodder guy an' he tell me if I want to matriculate. So I tell him no goddam way boy. Not here. So he tell me if I want to be soldier I have to go in nodder room an' matriculate wit six, seven odder guys. So I tell duh bugger *kitchisk*.

I don't want to be soldier dat goddam bad"

The Bootlegger — Part One

Rocky Poisson he get tired of robbing guys with no money, so he decide to be a bootlegger. But first he need some money, so he rob the priest an' he buy ten case of beer. Then he get a big tub an' a bunch of ice so he can have cold beer for the customers.

First guy to come along is Father Beaulieu, an' Poisson laugh when he see him. Anyways, Father Beaulieu he buy four case of beer an' he give Poisson twenty dollar then he tell him, "Let's have a beer." So he open a case an' they drink the whole thing. Then Poisson he feel a little bit guilty so he tell the priest, "Let's have one of mine." So they drink one case. Then one more. Then two more. Pretty soon they drink all Poisson beer 'cept for one case. Poisson he get too drunk an' he pass out but the priest he can still walk okay. He see his money is still on the table an' four case of beer is still left. So he take everthing an' he go home. So Poisson he wake up next morning an' all his money an' his beer is gone. He don't say nothing to nobody all week, but on Sunday he have to go to confession.

So he go into the confessional an' pretty soon they start whispering pretty loud in there. Everbody try to hear what they are saying. After a while we hear Poisson yell, "Fifteen goddam rosary? Jeeze crisse boy I don' kill nobody. All I do is steal some goddam money." Then Father Beaulieu yell, "Shut yer filty mout you dirty goddam matriculater." It get pretty quiet in there after that. Pretty soon the priest he come out an' he slam the door an' he go up an' he say mass.

But Poisson he stay in there all through mass. Miss communion too. When mass is over we all stay for fifteen, twenty minutes but Poisson he still don't come out so we all leave.

After that whenever the Priest see him he don't say nothing. He just jerk his hand at him a couple time

Roo Garoo
(for Alec Desmarais)

Lot of times bad things happen to good an' decent men. This is why we have to always show respect to everbody. All the time.

When some of the Old Peoples use to talk about Good an' Evil they always say it's the same guy. Take a look at a loonie. A one dollar. It have two sides. One side is the Queen an' other side is a loon. But it's still only one coin. Same thing with Good an' Evil. One guy but he have two sides to him. Old Peoples use to say when one is asleep, other one is awake right beside him

So. When Good is asleep, Evil he wakes up an' he sometimes takes a long look at a certain guy. Don't have to be a bad man. Maybe a guy who's a little bit too proud, or maybe he's not kind to the peoples who ain't as lucky as him. An' when Evil looks at him he says, "Now there's a guy who think he's too smart for me." So Evil, he says to himself, "I'm gonna give him a chance to get away from me. But I'm gonna make it so hard it might make him crazy." An' lot of guys do get crazy you know.

So Evil again he says to himself, "I'm gonna put a couple drops of poison in his blood an' I'm gonna turn him into something scary. Something that's gonna scare the peoples an' make them run away from him. At night I'm gonna change him into a Roo Garoo. A big scary black dog. That's right. A Roo Garoo. I'm gonna keep him up all night so he'll be tired all day an' he won't have no friends hardly. An' it's gonna be up to him to find somebody who ain't ascared of him. Somebody who's gonna be kind to him." But if you're kind to him when he's his self, it don't count. Only when he's a Roo Garoo. When he's big an' scary.

Then Evil again he says, "I'm gonna give him seven years. Ever night after dark I'm gonna change him into a Roo Garoo, an' when the sun comes up next morning I'm gonna change him back into a man. For seven years. An' when the sun come up on the very last morning, if he can't find nobody who's gonna be kind to him, I'm gonna come an' get him."

"But" Evil he says again, "With ever year that's pass I'm gonna give him less an' less time. For the last month I'm gonna give him only three, four hours an' maybe on only two nights a week. Two nights. When everbody is asleep. An' whoever is gonna be kind to him is gonna have to draw out the poison from his blood."

Now remember. Only the peoples who's gonna be kind to him can do that. But only when he's a Roo Garoo. Remember that too. An' the only way to draw out the poison in his blood is to cut him. On his left ear. An' if you don't have a knife or something else sharp you might even have to bite him. That's right. Bite him.

So this is how Evil works sometimes. If you're too proud or cheeky, he just might decide he wants to get a hold of you one day an' play tricks on you. Try an' make you crazy. This is why we always have to respect everbody. Be kind to everbody. 'Specially the peoples who ain't as lucky as us.

Kindness always beats Evil.

The Burden of Gratitude

The Old Peoples use to talk all the time about the right thing to do.

Was a story my grandfather use to tell about two guys, Pierre Bijou an' Gus MacDonald. They was best friends all the time. One day MacDonald's wife come to Bijou an' she tell him she's afraid her husband is a Roo Garoo. Well, Bijou he's like lot of peoples an' he laugh at stories like that. But she tell him that couple nights ago, she have to go over to the neighbour's place in the coulee an' borrow some tea. She says Gus is outside working when she leave, an' she tell him to boil some water so they can have tea when she come back. She says she's walking up the hill on the way back an' it's getting dark by now. All at once she sees a big black dog in front of her. His eyes are shining an' he have great big teeth. He's growling at her an' he won't get out the way, so she find a big stick an' she swing it at him. She miss him, an' he jump at her an' knock her down an' take a bite at her an' tear her dress before he run away. She run back home to tell Gus an' when she get there she can't find him nowhere. She says he's gone all night, an' in the morning she find him sleeping in the big chair an' he's got something stuck in his mouth between his teeth. She look closer an' here it's some threads from her dress. Well, she don't know what to do an' she's afraid to say something to him. So she go to Bijou for some help. Bijou he don't know what to do. He quit laughing an' he try to act like he's not ascared, so he tell her not to worry an' he'll think of something to do.

After that he start to hear some stories about lot of peoples see a big black dog at night. An' he start to think. He go an' talk to some Old Peoples an' they tell him that if you're going to help a guy who's a Roo Garoo, you gotta be kind to him an' you can't be ascared of him. They tell him it's a bad thing, an' the only way to help him is he have to draw blood, an' the only way to do that is to cut him on his left ear.

So Bijou at night he start to leave food around. He put fish beside his wood pile, or else a rabbit, a prairie chicken, a duck some times. In the morning the food is always gone, but whoever takes it don't leave no tracks. An' whenever he have to go some place at night he start taking a knife or a big sharp stick.

One night, Bijou he's walking home an' he hear something up ahead of him in the bush. He stop an' all at once he sees a big black dog in front of him on the path. The dog he's big an' ugly an' he's growling an' his eyes are shining. So Bijou he remember what the Old Peoples tell him an' he pull out his knife an' he walk towards the dog. The dog he jump at him an' knock him down, an' they roll around rassling on the ground. Bijou he gets bit and scratch pretty bad but after a while he cut the dog on his left ear before he pass out.

In the morning he wake up still in the bush, an' there's Gus sitting beside him, looks in pretty bad shape, his clothes is all torn and he have part of his ear missing. Gus ask him whattahell's going on, so Bijou tell him.

Well boy, after that, Gus he thank Bijou ever chance he get. He start buying him drinks at the beer parlour, buys him an' his wife presents, lends him money all the time. An' Bijou he thinks it's okay an' he take everthing what Gus give him.

This goes on for a couple years an' Gus he start to wonder about how long he have to thank Bijou. An' Bijou he start to get miserable sometimes, an' he start telling Gus he want more. He even start going over to Gus' house an' just takes stuff without even telling him or asking him. By this time Gus an' his wife they have three kids an' he can't afford to give Bijou stuff anymore. An' sure as hell can't lend him no more money. But Bijou he don't care. He tell Gus that if it wasn't for him, Gus would be in hell with *le Diable*. What can Gus do? He knows it's true.

But things get tougher an' tougher, an' one day Gus tells his wife that he's going to Bijou's place an' tell him he can't give him stuff no more, can't lend him money, an' he ain't gonna buy him no more drinks at the beer parlour. Well boy, they start talking an' pretty soon they get real mad at each other an' they start a fight. Bijou he end up falling an' hit his head on the corner of his stove an' he fall down dead.

Gus try to run away but it don't take too long for the police to find him an' he's charge with murder. It ends up they hang him. An' the two families they don't talk to each other no more. Never. An' they fight all the time. Even the grandchildren.

When the Old Peoples talk about it, they call it the burden of gratitude. When you do something for somebody, you're supposed to do it cause it's the right thing to do. An' when somebody thank you for being kind, it should be enough.

You never know when you might need somebody to be kind to you.

John Henry Rainville

You know, some guys they's just different. Not bad different. Good different. John Henry Rainville was a guy like that. Even when he was a boy. Lot of us guys we go to school until maybe grade five or six, enough so we learn how to read an' write okay, then we stay home an' help out, an' when we're old enough we find work. Me when I'm old enough I start working for guys. Farmers mostly, an' when I get a little older, I hire on to build roads or build elevators. John Henry he always work too but he always go back to school when the time come.

His dad was soldier in the first war, was wounded pretty bad an' he come back a pretty mean guy. Fight an' drink all the time, goes to jail a few times. Can't earn a good living. He die when John Henry is only a little boy, four-years-old.

John Henry's mother she make him promise always to go to school. Even when Depression come along he keep on an' his mother she hire out to do sewing an' cleaning for peoples who can afford to pay, an' they always have food on the table. An' John Henry, he turn out to be the kind of guy what takes care of things all the time. An' he don't fool around with the girls like the rest of us do. Oh the girls like him a lot, he treat them good but he's not like the rest of us. Me I say hello to a girl an' five minutes after we're in the bush. An' when we make a dance at somebody's place he don't get drunk an' fight. He dance with all the girls, he don't bother them, he even walks a couple of them home after. An' when we make a party down by the lake, he always make sure there's lots of wood an' he always make sure the fire's out after. Me too I help put the fire out after, but I'm too drunk lot of times an' I fall in an' they have to throw water on me instead of the fire.

When the war start he sign up right away. His mother she don't want him to go but he figgers he has to. He go overseas an' he write his mother a letter ever week, an' he save his money an' he send her a little bit all the time.

I don't know what he do in the war. He don't talk about it an' he come back same time as the rest of the guys. He have some money save up an' he fix up his mother's place on the road allowance. He buy her new stuff, dishes, some furniture, a new stove, stuff like that. He buy a cow an' a couple pigs an' some chickens. His mother, she make butter to sell an' when the chickens start to lay, they have eggs to sell too.

One day the priest come to their place, an' he tell them that since the war is over now they can start giving more for the collection in church. He tell them if they don't have money they can give butter an' milk an' eggs to the church.

Well, John Henry he tell that priest to go to hell an' he take him an' throw him out the house. Next day police come an' arrest him an' they send him to jail. For two years. He don't go to the jail in town but to the Pen. For two years. While he's in there he don't cause no trouble, he do his time. But about a year after he's in there, his mother die an' they don't even let him out for her funeral. He can't do nothing about it.

When he get out, he go back home an' there's nothing left. Nothing. All the windows is smashed, all his stuff is gone, even his stove. John Henry he don't have no money, an' by that time the govermint starts to move the peoples off the road allowances, so he have no where to go.

One day after that he's gone. Nobody see him no more an' nobody know where he's gone. Some peoples says he go up to the bush an' work but nobody know for sure.

I think about John Henry lot of times an' how things happen. Him, he have respect for everbody, don't ever hurt nobody, always ready to help somebody when they need it, an' stuff like that happen to him.

Don't make no sense boy. Don't make no sense.

St. Pierre's Granddaughter

I know there's a God. Has to be. B'cause when I ask Him for a granddaughter He send me you. Only one thing make me sad. Your *kokum* she not here to see you. You love her too if you see her.

Anyways, I have something to ask you. About Janvier. He have no grandchild. His wife an' his daughter they die with the fever. An' his two sons get kill in the war. He have nobody. Oh he act like a miserable old bugger sometimes. But it's okay. He is my best friend.

Anyways. He need a grandchild. So I wonder sometime it be okay you sit on his knee an' call him *mussom*. Then you can have two grandfathers, 'stead of just one.

Okay.

Bonne nuit ma joie. I love you.

Janvier's Lullaby

Janvier he want to give the baby a lullaby. So I give her to him he hold her in his arms an' he sing.

> *Poppa get the hammer*
> *Poppa get the hammer*
> *Poppa get the hammer*
> *There's a fly on Auntie's nose*

The baby she don't go to sleep. But she laugh.
That Janvier he's a crazy bugger sometimes.

THE ARMY WORMS
(for Joe Moran)

One summer the army worms was real bad. Eat everthing in sight boy. No leaves nowhere.

One day Janvier come to visit me. He bring me a beer an' we sit outside with my granddaughter. She play on the ground under a tree an' some worms they fall on the ground beside her.

She pick some up an' she going to eat them. Janvier he catch her before she put them in her mouth an' he tell her, "No no *ma vieille chouette*, don't eat them worms or else you get butterflies in your stomach."

The First Communion of Cecile Annette Marie Magdelaine St. Pierre — Part One

My granddaughter she have her first communion on Corpus Christie. But first she need a white dress an' a veil an' some shoes. So Janvier say he buy them for her.

So me an' him we go to the city an' find a big store. Have lot of stuff in it boy. A lady she come an' she ask to help. Janvier tell her, "Bonjour Mademoiselle, I am Tomas Albert Richard Janvier. My granddaughter she make it her first communion next Sunday an' she need to have a dress, a veil an' some shoes. White ones."

The lady she ask what size is my granddaughter. Janvier he look at me an' I shake my head, I don't know. So he tell her, "She is six-years-old, an' she have long black hair, an' big brown eyes an' freckles too. She is about this high an' have little tiny feet, an' she have two front teeth missing."

The lady she smile an' walk away. She have nice long legs boy an' Janvier watch her an' he smile. I think he forget about Rosalie Boyer for a while.

Pretty soon she come back an' she show it to us the stuff. Janvier look at them an' he tell her, "*Bon*." So she put them in a bag an' he give her the money an' she walk away again.

Janvier watch her some more an' he shake his head an' he look at me an' he say, "Hollasmokesboy, if she wrap them long legs around a guy I bet you she can squeeze a extra two, tree inches out of you for damn sure."

THE FIRST COMMUNION OF CECILE ANNETTE MARIE
MAGDELAINE ST. PIERRE — PART TWO

My granddaughter she have her first communion. When she walk down the aisle she smile at me. She make me think of her *kokum*. She go an' she kneel down an' she fold her hands an' she pray. So me too I pray.

I tell God it's okay He take her *kokum*, I see her again some day. Then I thank Him for my granddaughter.

Le Chien Du Pere Beaulieu
(for Joe Moran)

Father Beaulieu he come here in 1936. Can talk no English hardly. Not like me an' Janvier. He have a big ugly black dog. Look like a Roo Garoo.

Janvier he live right by the church an' one day the dog he have a shit on his yard. Janvier see him an' he come running out his porch an' he kick the dog an' he swear at him.

Father Beaulieu come running out the church an' he holler at Janvier, "*Pour quoi* you kick *mon chien* hon duh hass an' call him Fuck Off!"

After that whenever Janvier see the dog he tell him, "Come here Fuck Off."

Janvier Goes to Confession

Janvier he have to go to confession. On Sunday morning too. Before mass. If he tell the truth to Father Beaulieu he going to be in there a long time. He going to get five or six rosary for penance. An' kneeling down too.

He go an' visit with Rosalie Boyer last night. I think he was pretty busy guy too. That Rosalie she have big tits. An' Janvier he have small hands.

Janvier Makes a Picnic

Ever time Janvier make a picnic with Rosalie Boyer, he take Father Beaulieu dog with them. So one day I tell him, "How come you take Father Beaulieu dog with you ever time you make a picnic with Rosalie Boyer?"

So he tell me, "Flies. They use to bother me lots. So one day I think I like to borrow that ugly dog. The priest he think I like him an' he tell me. 'Don't call mon chien Fuck Off no more. His name is call Safranie.'"

So when we get to the picnic place I let him out an' he run around for a while. An' pretty soon I tell him, '*Domishi* Safranie'. So right away he go an' he have a shit. Oh about twenty-five, thirty feet away. Then we move the picnic up out the wind an' the flies they don't bother us no more."

Janvier's Cousin
(for Joe Moran)

Janvier he have a cousin, Modeste. Live up north in the bush all his life. One time he come down for a visit an' he meet everbody. He's a nice guy, gets along with everbody.

One day they have a baseball game. The guys from Jackrabbit Street play against the guys from the Coulee. First guy to bat for Jackrabbit Street hit the ball an' everbody yell, "RUN BOY RUN!" Next guy he hit the ball too an' everbody yell again.

Modeste he never see a ball game before an' he ask Janvier why everbody yell ever time somebody hit the ball. Janvier tell him everbody cheer at ball game. So next guy he hit the ball an' everbody yell again. Modeste too. Ever time somebody hit the ball he yell, "RUN BOY RUN!"

So Rocky Poisson he come up to bat one time an' the pitcher walk him, so he walk down to first base. Modeste he yell "RUN BOY RUN!" Janvier he tell him he don't have to run b'cause he have four balls. Modeste he say, "*Nom d'un chien*! Four balls?" Janvier tell him "Yeah boy, when a guy hit the ball he have to run but when he have four balls he can walk."

So Modeste he yell at Poisson, "WALK CAREFUL MY BOY. WALK CAREFUL."

The Bonspiel
(for Irene Moran)

One winter, Janvier, Rosalie Boyer, Rocky Poisson an' me, we have a team in the curling bonspiel. Good prizes too boy. First an' second place get money, an' third place get a toaster, a frying pan, a 'lectric mixer an' a bathroom scale.

We win third prize so me I don't care, I take the toaster an' Janvier he take the frying pan. But Rosalie an' Poisson the both of them they want the bathroom scale. So Poisson he grab it the bathroom scale an' he tell her, "You a woman, take duh mixer, it help you cook better. Besides I got no 'lectricity at my place."

So Rosalie grab it the scale from him an' she slap him an' she tell him, "*Mange le merde, Nono*! Whattahell you want a bathroom scale for? You going to have to put it by your slop pail."

Hungry Half Breed Song
(for Wannie Fisher)

There's worms in the porridge
There's ants in the jam
The bannock's all dried up
There's no lard in the pan
There's a mouse nest in the teapot
And bugs in the spam
There's flies in the buttermilk
But I don't give a damn

HALF BREED BREAKFAST
(for Alec Desmarais)

First you make the porridge. Nice an' thick boy. Put lot of brown sugar an' milk on it. Then you take two breads an' make a toast an' put lot of butter an' jam on. Eat that ever day boy, you gonna grow up an' be big strong hockey player. Just like Maurice Richard.

HALF BREED AIR CONDITIONING
(for Wannie Fisher)

You know what boy? When I am young man I work for farmers all the time. I have eight horses. That's my tractor. Farmers nowdays they drive them big goddam machines. Got tree hunderd an' fifty horses. Got air conditioning an' power steering too.

Lookit the wrists boy. Lookit the wrists. Can't get no wrists like that with power steering. Never lose a arm rassle in my life an' I'm sixty-two now.

Couple years ago, a big football player come down here from Regina. I take him down ten times in a row. Both hands boy. Both hands. I Indian rassle him too an' kick his ass all over the beer parlour. But he's a nice guy he buys me beer all night.

Anyways. Guys nowdays ride around all day on big air conditioning tractors. Me I have to walk behind the goddam plow all day. Only air conditioning I get is eight horses fart in my face.

How They Make Holy Water
(for Albert Bellerose)

You know how they make holy water boy? On Saturday after ever game the Montreal Canadiens play at the Forum, they melt the ice an' they put it in big tanks. Then they send it to the Pope an' he bless it, an' they send it out to all the churches. But whenever the Canadiens win the Stanley Cup, the Pope he don't have to bless it. They just send it out like that. This is true boy.

The 1949 Election

I am twenty-five that year. Strong like a horse too. Work ever day, even in the winter. Cutting wood, building fence. Stuff like that.

Election time come round that spring an' politicians was everwhere. Passing out beer an' promising everbody a job. The Conservateur he give me five dollar to vote for him. The Liberal he give me a case of beer. An' the CCF guy he don't give me nothing. But he say I can go on welfare. In the hard time he tell me. So me I take the five dollar an' the beer but I don't vote for nobody. I am drunk an' on welfare ever since.

Goddam Liberal. Goddam Conservateur. Goddam CCF.

How *Kokum* Emily and *Mussom* Zachary Brought Thanksgiving To Crooked Lake
(for Margaret Desjarlais)

At Crooked Lake once, was a poor family. Don't have no money an' no food. Thanksgiving was coming up. Was during '30s my boy, the husband can find no work round here. Hardly nobody can. Lots of the mans have to go away to find work. Have to hop freight train an' go sometimes a long way to find work. Even the white peoples.

So my husband an' me, we go an' see govermint man at the Fort an' we tell him bout this family, six, seven little ones, an' the woman is all alone. Husband is gone looking for work some place. Anyways, we tell govermint man an' he tell us he is take care of it. So we go home.

After two days pass my husband, Zachary his name is, he tell me he's going to Crooked Lake to see how things is. When he get back he is real mad, an' he tell me govermint man don't go to Crooked Lake, not even after two days pass. So me I get real mad an' I walk to town, all the way down the coulee, 'bout a mile an' a half. I go into the store at town an' I phone that dirty bugger. He tell me the woman have to make application, an' if she give false information he's going to put her in jail. I tell him she can't come all the way to town with seven little ones. It's more than ten miles. Besides I tell him, if you're going to put her in jail you're going to have to still feed them kids, an' you're going to have to pay a woman to come in there an' look after them. I ever give him hell my boy. 'Magine! He want to put a woman in jail b'cause she can't feed her kids. I get mad an' I tell him he is bloody well come out there with me an' I show him how much food she have. So he tell me okay, he come to get me tomorrow, an' we'll go there at dinner time an' we'll see what they have to eat.

Next morning I tell Zachary we bloody well fix that govermint man bugger. So I tell him first thing to get over to Crooked Lake, an' I give him half a bannock an' pail of lard to take along.

So govermint man he come to get me an' we go out to Crooked Lake. When we get there the woman an' her seven kids is all waiting. Oh they look pitiful. Like bunch of little orphans. I don't know where my husband is. He is hiding in bush some place he tell me after.

Govermint man, soon as he get in the house right away he is smell something cooking. So he tell me, "Look, they's a big pot of stew cooking on stove. These peoples they ain't starving." So he walk over to stove an' he lift the lid off pot an' he look in. Right away his eyes they get real big an' he turn real pale. White as a ghost my boy. My husband he kill seven little gophers an' he put theys head in pot, an' he cut theys mouth so it look like theys smiling. Govermint man he see those gophers head bouncing on top the water an' theys smiling at him. Just like seven little devils.

So right away I go to the cupboard an' my half a bannock an' lard is there, so I throw the bannock on table an' I slam the lard down an' I tell him, "That's all the bloody food they is. How do you like it if all you have to eat for Thanksgiving is gophers' head an' bannock?"

Right away he is run out to his car an' a few minutes later he is come back with voucher for $25. Then he even give her $10 out his own pocket to buy turkey an' some candies for kids. Oh he was ever upset. He don't say even one word. Nothing. All the way back.

Oh them govermint mans was real buggers some of them my boy. *Mon Dieu Salier.*

The Bootlegger — Part Two
(for Margaret Desjarlais)

Oh they is use to make some dandy party on Jackrabbit Street my boy. One time, was during Lent, the priest, Father Beaulieu, he hear about some peoples is going to make party on Saturday night, an' he get real mad an' he stand up in church an' tell us it's alright to make party but no liquor, b'cause it's Lent. He tell us it's MORTAL SIN an' everbody is go to hell who have liquor on Lent. This is true my boy. Right in church.

Anyways, Saturday night come an' lot of peoples was at party. St. Pierre he play fiddle an' Janvier is play guitar an' sing. Oh an' everbody is having good time, jigging, an' dancing, an' singing. 'Bout leven, leven thirty, some of the peoples say they wouldn't mind having little drink. Rocky Poisson was there, was dancing with Rose Adele Deuxchapeaux. A nice girl my boy, I don't know why she's dancing with that bugger all night. Anyways, Poisson leave party an' after 'bout half hour, he is come back an' he say he got ten case of beer an' some wine. Four gallon. He tell everbody it is cost lot of money so he's going to sell it to us.

Well nobody bring any money hardly 'cept Janvier. He have twenty dollar bill an' he tell Poisson he is buy case of beer for his self an' sealer of wine for Rosalie Boyer. Poisson tell him case of beer is cost five dollar an' sealer of wine is one dollar. Altogether it makes six dollar he want. So Janvier give him twenty dollar an' tell him he want fourteen dollar back change. But Poisson he have no change so he tell Janvier he give him change tomorrow. Janvier tell him *"Kitchisk."* So then he tell Poisson he'll mark it down on piece of paper, an' he sign it an' Poisson sign it, an' it's just like legal piece of paper. Besides, he tell Poisson, "Everbody here is witness." Poisson he think for while an' finally he say okay.

So after Janvier get his wine an' his beer, he wait 'til Poisson is not looking an' he give the twenty dollar to my husband. He go to Poisson an' tell him same thing. They sign paper an' Zachary get case of beer for his self an' sealer of wine for me. Then Zachary give the twenty dollar to somebody else. That twenty dollar pass through everbody's hands, an' pretty soon everbody is have beer an' wine, an' Poisson he have paper what all the peoples signs, so he start to act like *Gros boque*, an' he start to drink too. When party is over Poisson is pass out. Janvier he see the paper with all the peoples names, so he take it an' he burn it, an' everbody is go home because there's church in morning.

When Poisson get to church in morning, he is not look too happy an' he go an' sit by his self. Anyways, mass is take long time to start, an' pretty soon the priest come down an' he whisper something to St. Pierre. After while St. Pierre go over to Poisson an' tell him four gallon of wine is missing from church, an' the priest want to know if he can borrow some wine for mass. Poisson he is get big smile on his face an' say sure, he have a gallon left over an' the priest can have it for fifty dollar. What can the priest do? He need wine to say mass so he have to give Poisson fifty dollar.

For sermon the priest talk about stealing an' he is look at Poisson all the time. Poisson is just sit there an' smiling an' ever once in while he jerk his hand at the priest.

Oh what a dirty bugger that Poisson is my boy.

Gunther Primeau

Gunther. I wonder wherenahell a Half Breed get a name like that. Gunther. Well anyways, one time he buy a car, a DeSoto, I don't know what year but Jeeze Chrisse it's a long car. Can have a square dance in there just about. Well you know him, he have a job an' money in his pocket all the time.

But he can't find no woman. Womans don't like him. He drive the honey wagon an' he stink like the lagoon all the time. So he tell me once if I can help him find a woman. So me I tell him first he's gotta wash. I tell him, "Jeeze Chrisse boy, you can't get no woman if you stink like the goddam slop pail all the time. And your car. Wash your car too." An' you know what else? Even his money it stink. You won't believe it, one time he pay me a beer in the beer parlour with a five dollars. Hollasmokesboy, I just about have to go outside an' throw up that five dollars it stink so bad. An' I tell him, "Buy some new clothes too. Jeeze Chrisse boy you have a job."

So anyways, Saturday night come along an' we go to a dance. Old Gunther he's all dress up an' clean. Looks pretty good. He don't stink. His car it don't stink. An' his money it don't even stink. It's true. He even go to the bank an' get some new money. But you know that stupid bugger? I introduce his name to a couple nice womans. Real good looking too. Eva Lajeunesse an' Doris Charbonneau. An' Eva she look real good. She have on a black dress an' red shoes with the heels behind. But you know, he don't want to talk. He don't want to dance. All he wants to do is drink all night. He get so drunk he pass out before midnight.

After dance is over, Eva an' Doris want a ride home. They say they want to make a party too. So me I look at Gunther an' he's pass out still, so I take his keys an' I leave him there. Me an' the two womans we take his car an' we go get some beer from the bootlegger an' we go make a party at their place.

Next morning come an' I wake up an' there's a guy standing there. He tell me, "How much you want for your car?" So me right away I gotta think. I know Gunther pay only four hunderd dollars so I tell the guy, "Nine hunderd." An' he say, "Five hunderd." So I say, "Seven fifty. Cash money. An' a ride home." Well you know that bugger, he pull out of his pocket nearly a thousand dollars. Wha wha boy I just about choke. I should of told him at least eight hunderd, but I take the seven fifty. Then I tell him if it's okay I make bill of sale for five hunderd. He don't care so he give me a ride home.

Well you know, I go over to Gunther's place an' I tell him I sell his car for him, an' I slap down on the table five hunderd dollars an' bill of sale. Well Jeeze Chrisse boy he get mad. He call me *enfant chiene*, an' he want his goddam car back, an' if he don't get it he's going to call police. So I tell him, "Jeeze Chrisse boy, you pay only four hunderd dollars for the goddam thing an' I make you a extra hunderd dollars. Whattahell you mad for? It's a damn good deal I make." He tell me gettahell out his house.

Next day policeman come to where I'm working an' he arrest me for stealing Gunther's car an' selling it illegal. Hollafuckboy, I have to even hire a lawyer! It cost me two hunderd an' fifty dollars but they send me to jail anyway! For nine months! Jeeze Chrisse am I ever mad at that goddam Gunther. So I have to do my nine months. But it's not too bad, I know everbody in there just about.

So after nine months pass I get out. Got no money. No job. I'm walking along an' all at once I see a big brand new DeSoto coming. An' here it's that goddam Gunther an' he's got two womans with him. Eva Lajeunesse an' Doris Charbonneau. They just drive by. Don't even look at me.

It's the last goddam time I do that bugger a favour.

The German Woman

You know, I use to make sex with prostitutes. Not all the time, during the war mostly. Whattahell boy, there's a war on an' I figger some German guy he's gonna try an' kill me first chance he get. So me I figger I'm gonna be with a woman ever chance I get. Even if I gotta pay her. An' lots of times not even to make sex. Just to be with a woman.

One time, in Germany towards the end, I meet a woman in a beer parlour. Real skinny an' old too, maybe about forty-five, fifty. Well it's not old now but in them days I'm just a young man, twenty-four, twenty-five-years-old. Anyways I meet this German woman, her name was call Helga or Hilda or something. I buy her glass of whiskey an' we start talking. She talk pretty good English but me I don't talk no German. All at once she tell me if I want to make sex with her. For a dollar. I figger whattahell so I buy a small bottle of whiskey an' we walk to her place. It's not far.

So we get to her place an' you won't believe it. She live in a old church, all the windows is smashed an' the doors is missing an' half the walls is caved in. Garbage, an' skinny dogs, an' old cars all over the place. Jeeze Chrisse boy I never seen no place like that before.

An' stink! Hollamoses! It smell like piss an' shit an' rotten cabbage. An' there's no furniture. Nothing. Not even no pews. An' there's two kids sitting in the middle of the floor. Musta been seven, eight years old. They was eating rotten potato peelings out of a garbage can. Honest to God boy you won't believe it. They was so goddam skinny I could see all their bones through their skin. An' there's a old skinny guy on a mattress over by the window. At first I think he's dead but all at once I hear him groaning. It's the priest the woman tell me. An' she don't know whose the two kids are. She don't know even where her husband is. He's a German soldier an' she thinks the Russians prob'ly kill him.

Anyways, she walk up behind the altar an' she tell me if I want to go behind there with her. I look at them two kids an' the priest. Then her. An' me I don't say nothing. I put ten dollars in her hand an' I gettahell out of there. In a goddam hurry too.

I can never forget them two kids. An' that skinny old priest.

An' the German woman.

'Ti Boy — Part One

Pascal LaViolette. 'ti Boy we use to call him. His dad was call Old LaViolette, an' his grandfather Old, Old LaViolette. Old, Old LaViolette, he talk li- li- like thi- this all th- th- ti- ti- time. An' his hands shake too. He use to get me an' my sister to take him across the river all the time, in our boat. Use to walk down the hill with two gunny sacks. We can hear bottles go CLINK CLINK CLINK inside the gunny sacks. Oh I know he's a bootlegger. He use to take his stuff to town an' sell it all the time. He can't take his team with his hands shakin' all the time or else he's make his poor horses crazy. He hide a wheel barrow in the bush on other side of the river. Then when he get out our boat he just put his whiskey in there an' he walk to town. He use to pay me an' my sister fifty cents, an' when he come back from town he give us candy, an' sometimes he bring us a Coca Cola.

Anyways, I meet up with him one time, 'ti Boy. In Italy. Was with the Signals, a radio operator. One day he tell me he want to go to town. He seen some nice girls there walkin around, an' he tell me if I can lend him ten dollars. He says he haven't been with a woman since Montreal. Me I have only ten dollars an' I wanna go to town too, so I can't lend him no money.

Anyways, on church parade one Sunday a couple weeks after, a priest from town come an' we all go to confession. An' me I'm right behind 'ti Boy, so I figger I'm gonna play him a trick an' listen to him an' the priest. So I get real close an' I hear him tell the priest, "Bless me Father, it's two weeks since I have confession last time." Then he say, "Excuse me Father, but I make sex with the both of them my hands five times." An' the priest he says, "*Five* times! With the both of them your hands?" An' me I'm starting to laugh like a bugger. Then 'ti Boy tell the priest, "No, no Father. Not the both of them at the same time. Five times with one hand each." So the priest he says, "Five times with each one of them your hands? How come you don't use the same hand all the time?" An' 'ti Boy he says, "I don't know, that's the way I learn how to do it." An' the priest says, "Whonahell teach you how to do it that way?" An' 'ti Boy he's getting mad at that nosey priest an' he tell him, "Whattahell difference it makes?" Then the priest he ask him, "What hand you write with?" An' 'ti Boy he's real mad by now an' he tell the priest, "None of your goddam business." An' the priest says, "Well you gotta know how to write if you join the army." So 'ti Boy tell him, "I write with the both of them my goddam hands too." Then the priest say, "Five times with each of them your hands! That's a lot of goddam sex. Boy yer a dirty pig." So for penance he give poor 'ti Boy ten rosaries.

So me I don't want to spend the next three months saying the rosary, so I don't tell him I listen to 'ti Boy have confession, an' I make sex with two womans, an' have a fight with three Americans. Instead I tell him I say bad words an' lie to my sergeant. An' he give me only three Our Fathers an' three Hail Marys.

I figger whattahell, it's okay to kill Germans an' Italians an' you don't have to go to confession for that.

So me I just lie to the bugger an' say my penance.

'Ti Boy — Part Two

You know. In the war I kill only four guys. That's all. Four. In Italy on Thanksgiving one time, me an' 'ti Boy was gonna try an' steal a turkey. But they got no turkeys over there I don't think. We can't find one. So 'ti Boy instead he steal a goose an' he's gonna cook it for Thanksgiving. While he's cooking it somebody says it be nice if we have some wine. So me I take a Jeep an' I go to town. I know a guy there who have a lot of wine at his place. He give me five bottles an' I don't even have to pay him. On the way back all at once I hear, WHOOM! WHOOM! WHOOM! Mortars. We all know the Germans is not far away but they don't bother us for three weeks almost. Oh maybe a sniper once in a while but they don't hit nobody. Just try an' scare us a little bit. But me I hurry back anyway an' when I get there, them goddam Germans, they put three mortars right in our camp. They blow up our signals truck, a machine gun an' our mess tent. Eight guys killed. 'ti Boy too. All blowed apart an' his guts coming out his belly. An' his face is gone. He got no face. An' you know what? All I can think about is he owe me a chocolate bar. A Hershey bar.

In town the peoples all the time talk about some German officers come to the café to eat an' get drunk once in a while. So I tell the sergeant I'm going back to town an' I might not be back for couple days. Well boy. I wait around that place for three days. The woman there who own the place she keep me an' feed me.

Third night come along an' sure as hell, a big black car come along an' three Germans get out. Officers. That's not all. That priest is with them. I have my bayonet an' I wait an' I wait. After a few hours pass they come out. Drunk an' laffing. An' singing. An'. Well.

That goddam priest I kill him too an' I don't give a damn even if I have to go to hell for that. I'll be there right beside that bastard. I put them in their car an' I drive it three, four miles outside town. Toward their lines. I spill gas all over them an' I set the car on fire an' I burn the bastards.

Ever see your friend dead? No arms? No legs? No face?

Q Pontoon

When the war start I join up right away. They think I'm a pretty smart guy so they put me with the Engineers. Building bridge, roads, demolitions. Everthing like that. We have to go to England to take training. The instructors is all Englishmans an' they's call QMSI. I don't know what that means. QMSI. But they have them instead of Sergeant Major in England. Everbody call them Q.

This one guy, we have him for bridge building an' we call him Q Pontoon. One day he's showing about thirty, thirty-five us guys how to take apart a anti-tank mine. He tell us not to worry if we step on one because it takes a fifty-ton tank to make one explode. It's all right he tell us. It's okay. So just to show us, he set one down on the floor an' he get up on a table an' he jump.

Hollasmokesboy! That goddam thing explode an' it kill Q an' thirty other guys an' blow the whole goddam building all to hell. Me an' four other guys was sitting in the back an' it don't even hurt us. I don't know why. Oh it knock us out for three, four minutes but that's all.

An' the goddam mess. Only thing left of Q is his right boot, an' part of his leg an' his foot left in it. An' you know the thing I remember most? He's wearing one of them Argyle socks with one of them little garters holding it up.

Q Pontoon.

Was a good lesson he teach me.

The English Patient

After the war I volunteer to stay in Germany. Help to train guys for the Occupation. Me I'm a Sergeant now. It's true. I get my stripes just before Holland. You know what? I go through the whole goddam war an' I don't get hurt even once. I don't get wounded. I don't get a scratch. A goddam mosquito don't even bite me. Yeah boy it's true. Oh I get shot at lots of times but I don't know why everbody miss me. But two months after the war I get shot in the ass. Right across both my fesses.

We was giving live ammunition training to some new guys. You crawl on your belly in a trench an' a guy with a machine gun shoots over you. Oh maybe a foot, sometimes less even, 'specially if the machine gun guy is a asshole. One time this one guy, a big dumb guy, I don't know where he's from, he can't keep his ass down so me I gotta show him. But first I tell the machine gun guy, "Don't shoot too low." So I get on my belly an' I start to crawl in the trench.

All at once I see a great big rat smiling at me. He's so goddam big at first I think he's a wiener dog. That's how big he was that bugger. An' his tail it must be a goddam foot long, an' all at once he start to crawl towards me. Jeeze Chrisse boy, he come at me an' he's smiling at me. Hollasmokes! I just about shit on my pants. I jump up an' I start yelling an' all at once a bullet come an' hit me right on the ass. Right across both my fesses. Lucky thing it miss my ass bone an' everthing. You ever see one of them bullets? A fifty caliber? Big as a goddam Coca Cola bottle just about.

I start yelling an' waving my arms but that stupid bugger machine gun guy, I don't know whattahell is going on with him. He keep on shooting! Yeah! He keep on going to the right an' when he get to the end he start coming back. An' me I'm still yelling an' waving my arms an' everthing. But him he don't quit shooting an' he's getting closer an' closer. Me I don't want to get shot so I start running. About a hunderd yards away is a ravine, so I start running there an' at the same time I'm holding on to my ass. An' that stupid bugger he keep on shooting. An' them bullets theys hitting all around me. WHUNK! WHUNK! WHUNK! An' me I'm running like this an' like that. Like a jackrabbit when your dog is chasing him. So about ten feet from the ravine I say to hell with it an' I make a hellova leap. But I forget the ravine there is real steep, straight down almost. But I don't give a damn no more an' I jump anyways an' I bounce down all the way an' I knock myself out.

Next thing I know I wake up in the hospital an' it feels like somebody put a setaline torch on my ass. Jeeze Chrisse boy it hurt. An' burn! An' here I got my arms stuck up in the air an' they's hitched up to a pulley over the bed. Yeah boy. I break my arms too. The both of them. I have to stay like that 'til a couple weeks pass then they send me to a hospital in England. A real hospital. Nice place too. Lot of nice nurses but I can't do nothing. I'm like that for two months almost. Somebody even have to feed me all the time.

But that's nothing. You ever try an' have a shit laying on your back? Yeah! They have to lift me up and stick a pan under me. A bread pan or something they call it. An' they stand there an' watch 'til you're finished. You ever try an' have a shit with ten people watching you? An' one of them even have to wipe my ass for me.

An' that's not all! One day a doctor come an' tell me he's afraid I might have gangrene, an' he's afraid my ass is gonna to rot off. An' never mind. He tell me they's gonna have to put maggots on my ass to eat the rotten part! It's true! So they unhook my arms an' roll me over on my belly an' they stick a bunch of maggots on my ass. Yeah! How you gonna like it if you have to lay on your belly like that with two broken arms an' maggots crawling all over your ass? Never mind that. How you gonna like it if you have to shit upside down? An' what happens if one of them goddam maggots decide he's gonna crawl up your ass?

I'm like that for two months just about 'til it start to heal. An' the nurses they make jokes all the time. One of them tell me if someone make a line across my ass an' two down, they can play X an' O's. The other one say that's no good because the guy who have O have to start in the middle all the time.

Mary Margaret Francine Striker Jones

In England I have a girlfriend. Oh she's a good looking woman. She have red hair, an' green eyes, an' cute little freckles on her knees. An' oh she ever have nice long legs. She have lot of names too. Mary, an' Margaret, an' Francine, an' Striker, an' Jones. But I just call her Jonsey. That's too damn many names for one woman. I buy her nylons all the time. An' a garter belt too. A purple one.

Me I want to marry her an' I want to buy her a ring. She tell me she already have a ring. A diamond. Her grandmother give it to her. So I buy her a necklace an' ear rings instead. Amber. She pick them out herself.

They ship me out a couple weeks after an' I can't go see her, so I write her a letter an' tell her I love her, an' we have to wait 'til after the war. I tell her I write her all the time from wherever I am. You know, I write her letters from everplace. North Africa. Italy. France. Holland. Germany. Everplace. But I never get back even one letter from her. Not one. An' I don't see her again 'til I get out the hospital after I get shot on the ass.

In the hospital I meet a guy. American. Was a sergeant too. In the Airborne. We both have about a month before they ship us home. After we get out the hospital we go to a pub an' pretty soon we start talking about English girls. He tell me he use to have a girlfriend. Says he use to buy her nylons, an' garter belts, an' perfume. He even buy her a ring. A diamond. But they ship him out before he can marry her. He tell me he write her letters from all over the place but not once did he get back a letter from her. Then he tell me, "Oh Jeeze Chrisse boy she's a beautiful woman. Red hair. Green eyes. An' long, long legs." Then he tell me her name. Hollasmokesboy! We just about have another war right there in that pub. Lucky thing some big Polish guys was in there to stop us. So we get drunk with the Polish guys instead of fight.

But you know, a couple weeks pass an' I read in a newspaper that they was sending a whole bunch of C rations to Germany for the Occupation. Me I have nothing to do so I figger I'll go watch them load it up an' say good riddance. Boy that was awful stuff, 'specially herrings in tomato sauce. The English guys they call it Herrings In. An' Bully Beef! Hollasmokesboy! I rather eat a raw gopher.

So anyways, I go down to the airstrip an' there's a general there. American. He's getting his picture took beside a great big bunch of boxes of Herrings In. I guess the load wasn't packed too tight an' all at once the bindings come loose an' the whole goddam load come falling down on top of him. Kill the poor bugger.

So next week in the newspaper I see a picture of Jonsey. It says she's a grieving widow. The American General is her husband! So just for the hell of it I look up her phone number, to see if she want to talk to me. You know what? She laugh like hell when she find out it's me. Then she invite me over to her place. Wha wha she ever have a nice house. A butler an' everthing. She's all dress up in black, says she's in mourning. But I stay with her for a week.

She tell me she's married when the war start. To a pilot. RAF. He get killed early on an' they give her widow's pension. She says it's okay, enough that she don't have to go to work. Then she marry up with another RAF guy. An' him too he get shot down an' she get some more widow's pension. Well boy. She figger it's a hellova deal so she marry another pilot. American this time. An' sure as hell the poor bugger he get shot down. Then again. Another American. She says she don't want to marry another English guy. She's afraid they might catch on. So she marry two Americans. They get better pay an' better pensions. So after the second American, she figger she have enough husbands an' enough pensions an' she don't want to push her luck no more, so she quit marrying everbody.

So I ask her how come she fool around with guys like me but marry up with pilots all the time. She says they get better pension an' they don't last too long. But she have more fun with guys like me.

Then I ask her how come she get engage with me an' she says she get engage with five other guys too. Well, what can I do? I can't get mad at a woman who have red hair, an' green eyes, an' cute little freckles, an' long legs. Jeeze Chrisse boy!

So then I ask her about the general. She says she really love this one an' he's gonna take her back to the States. California. But he get kill by the Herrings In, an' she's getting some more pension, an' she figger she don't want no more husbands, an' she's gonna stay in England.

Poor Jonsey.

Seven-Toed Pete

When I was a boy, nine, ten-years-old, was a old Chinaman, Pete, owned the café. I don't know his last name, everbody call him Seven-toed Pete. He always play poker with the old guys an' it's his favorite game. Four up, three down, low in the hole wild.

One morning he's in his café all alone, an' I go in there an' I steal a chocolate bar. O Henry. Cost five cents. I run out the café and he chase me. Boy that old bugger can run fast, he catch me before I get a half a block. But you know, he don't tell my mother. Instead he make me pick up papers an' stuff in front of the café, then he let me keep the chocolate bar. So ever day after that I always go clean up in front of the café, an' twice, sometimes three times a week, he give me a chocolate bar. An' on Saturdays sometimes, he give me a twenty-five cents to go to picture show. It cost ten cents to get in an' I can buy popcorn and Coca Cola too.

One day, I musta been fourteen, I seen some older boys go in and they rub their finger across their teeth an' they run like hell. Old Pete he chase them down the street with a baseball bat, but he can't catch them. Lot of guys use to do that to them old Chinamans. They rub their finger across their teeth then laugh an' run like hell. I don't know what it means but it sure make Pete mad.

You know, I do some stupid things in my life, but the stupidest thing I ever do is try that on Pete. Yeah. One day. Was after school. I was pickin' up some papers in front and I don't know what make me do it. I go inside, Pete's in there at the counter so I call him. He look up at me an' I do it. I don't know what make me do it boy. I just don't know. As soon as I do it I know I do something stupid.

You know that Pete? He don't do nothing. He just look at me. Just look at me. Pretty soon I see tears coming down his cheeks. He don't say nothing. He just stare at me for a while then he go an' sit down with his back to me. I stand there for a while an' I try to tell him I'm sorry but I can't talk. I start to cry an' Pete he just stay there with his back to me. I turn around an' I walk out an' I never go back. Never.

Pete never talk to me again. Never. Even when I join up to go overseas I can't go to his place an' tell him goodbye.

But you know, in Italy at Christmas, I get a parcel from home. It's from Pete. I open it up an' it's a whole box of chocolate bars. O Henrys. He write me a letter too. He tell me he's sorry he don't talk to me all those years. He tell me when I get back home he's going to make a big party for me. Jeeze Chrisse boy I'm so happy I start to cry. Then a couple months after I get a letter from home. From my mother. She tell me Pete die. Cancer.

I can never forget that old man. An' what I do to him.

Seven-toed Pete.

Little Petey
(for Pte. Pete Johnson PPCLI)

Little Petey was eleven-years-old when the war is over. He have two big brothers. They get back from Europe just before Thanksgiving 1945. They wear their uniforms an' have lot of medals on their chest. They was combat soldiers. Officers. Everbody's happy when they get back an' have a big party for them. They was heroes an' Little Petey was real proud, an' he tell everbody that when he get big he's going to be soldier too.

When Korea start he's sixteen-years-old, an' one day we don't see him no more. He quit school an' he tell his parents he's going away to find work. Lot of young guys do that in them days. I guess he go to the city an' he lie about his age an' he join up in the Army, an' he get sent to Korea. An' he's not even seventeen yet. One day his mother an' dad they get a letter from the govermint. Little Petey is prisoner of war an' they don't know where he is. Some place in North Korea or China maybe. So right away they write back an' say he's not old enough to be soldier. But is too late.

You know. Little Petey he have a big poche an' everbody tease him all the time, how he's going to make lot of womans happy when he's old enough. Petey is real shy about it an' sometimes he get mad. But it's only teasing.

Anyways. In prison camp the guy in charge find out about Petey. Lot of times he make him stand outside with his poche hanging out an' everbody make fun of him. One day he bring a little Korean girl to camp. Little Petey is standing out there with his poche hanging out an' camp commander tell Petey to fuck her. Well he's not going to do that an' he tell camp commander "No." That guy he get the guards to knock Petey down an' they kick him an' smash him an' poke him with their rifles, but Petey still say "No." So they put him in little barbwire cage in the ground. Petey can't move. He can just lay there on his belly, an' there's rats an' lizards an' spiders an' everthing in that hole with him. An' they don't feed him anything hardly. Ever day for a week this happen. An' the little girl she's scared an' she cry all the time.

After a week pass, camp commander he hold a pistol at little girl's head, an' he tell Petey if he don't do it, he's going to shoot her. What can Petey do? He's not even seventeen yet. He don't want little girl to die. So he do it. Camp commander an' all the guards they yell an' laugh. Poor little girl an' Petey all alone out there on the ground. When he's finish they lay there an' they's both crying. Little girl she's bleeding all over. She's all tore up. Camp commander, he stand her up an' he shoot her anyway an' he tell Petey he's got to bury her. Petey he have to dig a hole an' put the little girl in an' cover her up. He lay on top of her grave an' he cry for three days, until they come an' get him an' put him back in the cage.

When the war is over they send him back an' they put him in the crazy house. His parents go to visit him once an' Petey he don't even know them. He just sit there in a little room. Cries all the time. They go back a few more times but it's no use. He stays the same. He stay in that place for twenty-five years almost. Sometime around 1975, '76, around there, govermint says they's going to move everbody out. They's going to close down all the crazy houses. They move Petey to the city. Put him on welfare an' they find a place for him in a boarding house. One of them places downtown, dirty all the time, cold in the winter, hot in the summer. Place stinks all the time.

When Petey get his welfare check he go down to the beer parlour. One of the rough places where the Indians an' Half Breeds drink all the time. An' he act crazy all the time an' everbody laugh at him. Buys everbody beer an' cigarettes 'til his money's all gone. Then he's got no money, an' you know what he have to do for beer an' cigarettes? They make him take out his poche an' put it in beer pitcher an' they pour beer in an' he drink it. Oh an' they all laugh at him how crazy he is.

Even the womans do it. Then when he get another welfare check he start all over again.

One night he get drunk an' he go home an' he fall asleep with a cigarette that's still going. He get burn up pretty bad in the fire an' they's not very much left of him. So the govermint pay his funeral an' everbody forget about him.

You know, lot of bad things happens to some peoples. 'Specially in the war. Lot of guys suffer like Petey. But guys like me we go through a whole war an' nothing like that happen to us. Why? We get medals an' everbody call us heroes. But what about Petey? He's a damn better hero than me that's for sure.

But you know what bother me just as much as what happen to him? The way we treat him after. His own peoples an' we treat him like he don't count no more. When he get home we don't take him back. An' he belong to us. We let govermint stick him in the crazy house so he can rot away his life.

Lot of peoples blame the govermint, but they have to do something. We won't.

The Seasons

Winter, my *mussom* Pollock
gave us his blessing on New Year's Eve
Then he told us stories
A story my grandfather gave me this

Spring, my *kokum* Veronique, before she died
I put on my Mussom's hat, put his pipe in my mouth
and I walked into her room and she laughed
Laughter my grandmother gave me this

Summer, my mother Marian, sang to me
while she rubbed my back
because the mosquitoes bit me
A song my mother gave me this

Autumn, my father Little Joe, took us
to an orphanage after our mother died
He cried when he left us
Lonesome my father gave me this

Mon Cousin
(for Lloyd Fisher)

Cheetah. *Mon cousin.*

On the day I started school I found a dime and a fat guy tried to take it from me. So *mon cousin* gave him a licken. Then at recess we sneaked to the store and we bought a whole bunch of jaw breakers and purple ice cream. We got hell but we didn't care.

Me and *mon cousin.*

Pee Wee
(for Ralph Blondeau)

Pee Wee is the mayor now. When me and six of my brothers and sisters were sent away to an orphanage after our mother died, he wrote me a letter and he taped a quarter to it. I hung on to that quarter for about three weeks until I lost it. Just about forty years later I still remember this. So I ask Pee Wee if he still remembers. He says he does, but then he tells me the quarter wasn't for me. It was for my brother Danny.